CROCODILE'S BAG

Cast of Characters

 Narrator

 Girl

 Crocodile

 Boy

 Woman

 Grandmother

 Man

ACT ONE

 Narrator: One morning, a clever crocodile went swimming in the Zambezi River and caught a fish.

 Crocodile: One little fish will not feed a big crocodile like me, but I am a clever crocodile, I have a plan, a clever plan.

 Narrator: So the clever crocodile put the fish in a bag and tied it closed with a vine. He walked to the village and stopped at the first hut.

3

 Crocodile: Good morning, Woman. May I leave my bag with you while I go swimming?

 Woman: Yes, you may.
(She takes the bag.)

 Crocodile: Whatever you do, don't open the bag.

There's a surprise inside.

(The crocodile turns and walks away.)

5

 Narrator: As soon as the crocodile was gone, the woman looked at the bag.
She shook it and felt it.
She smelt it, but she could not guess what was inside.

Woman: I wonder what kind of
surprise is in the bag.
Maybe I'll just take
a little peek.
(She looks into the bag.)

Narrator: When she untied the vine,
the fish flipped out,
and the woman's rooster flew down
and swallowed it whole.
Not long after that,
the crocodile returned
from his swim.

Crocodile: *(He looks into the bag.)*
Where is my fish?

7

Woman: I opened the bag, and the fish flipped out. Then my rooster swallowed it.

8

Crocodile: Then I will have to take the rooster.
(He puts the rooster into the bag.)

 Narrator: So the crocodile went down the road to the second hut.

 Crocodile: Good morning, Man. May I leave my bag with you while I go swimming?

 Man: Yes, you may.
(He takes the bag.)

 Crocodile: Whatever you do,
don't open the bag.
There's a surprise inside.
(The crocodile turns and walks away.)

 Narrator: As soon as he was gone,
the man looked at the bag.
He shook it and felt it.

He smelt it, but he could not
guess what was inside.

 Man: I wonder what kind of
surprise is in the bag.
Maybe I'll just take
a little peek.
(He looks into the bag.)

 Narrator: When he untied the vine,

the rooster flew out,

and the man's cat jumped up

and swallowed it whole.

 12

ACT TWO

 Narrator: Pretty soon, the crocodile returned from his swim.

 Crocodile: *(He looks into the bag.)* Where is my rooster?

 Man: I opened the bag, and the rooster flew out. Then my cat swallowed it.

 Crocodile: Then I will have to take the cat. *(He puts the cat into the bag.)*

Narrator: So the crocodile went down the road to the third hut.

 Crocodile: Good morning, Girl. May I leave my bag with you while I go swimming?

Girl: Yes, you may.

(She takes the bag.)

 Crocodile: Whatever you do,

don't open the bag.

There's a surprise inside.

(The crocodile turns and walks away.)

Narrator: As soon as he was gone, the girl looked at the bag. She shook it and felt it. She smelt it, but she could not guess what was inside.

16

Girl: I wonder what kind of
surprise is in the bag.
Maybe I'll just take
a little peek.
(She looks into the bag.)

 Narrator: When she untied the vine,
the cat climbed out,
and the girl's dog jumped up
and swallowed it whole.
Not long after that,
the crocodile returned
from his swim.

 Crocodile: *(He looks into the bag.)*
Where is my cat?

 Girl: I opened the bag,
and the cat jumped out.
Then my dog swallowed it.

 18

Crocodile: Then I will have to take the dog.
(He puts the dog into the bag.)

 Narrator: So the crocodile went down the road to the fourth hut.

 Crocodile: Good morning, Boy. May I leave my bag with you while I go swimming?

 Boy: Yes, you may.
(He takes the bag.)

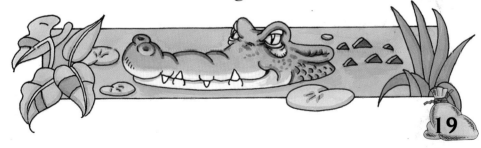

Crocodile: Whatever you do, don't open the bag. There's a surprise inside.

(The crocodile turns and walks away.)

 Narrator: As soon as he was gone, the boy looked at the bag. He shook it and felt it. He smelt it, but he could not guess what was inside.

 Boy: I wonder what kind of surprise is in the bag. Maybe I'll just take a little peek.

(He looks into the bag.)

 Narrator: When he untied the vine, the dog jumped out, and the boy's goat chased it away down the hill.

ACT THREE

Narrator: Pretty soon, the crocodile returned from his swim.

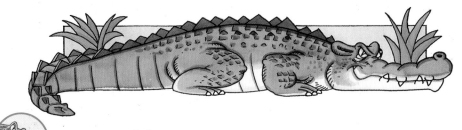

Crocodile: *(He looks into the bag.)* Where is my dog?

Boy: I opened the bag, and the dog jumped out. Then my goat chased it away down the hill.

Crocodile: Then I will have to take the goat.

(He looks around for the goat.)

 Boy: My goat has not come back.

 Crocodile: Then I will have to take you!

Narrator: The crocodile put the boy in the bag. After a while, he decided to stop at one more hut.

 Crocodile: Good morning, Grandmother. May I leave my bag with you while I go swimming?

 Grandmother: Yes, you may.
(She takes the bag.)

 Crocodile: Whatever you do, don't open the bag. There's a surprise inside.
(The crocodile turns and walks away.)

 24

 Narrator: As soon as the crocodile was gone, the grandmother studied the bag. She shook it and felt it. She smelt it.

Grandmother: I know what's in the bag!

(She opens the bag.)

 Narrator: She untied the vine, and the boy popped out. Then the grandmother decided to teach the crocodile a lesson. She put her pet python in the bag and tied the bag shut.

Boy: Let's hide behind the hut and see what happens.
(The boy and his grandmother hide behind the hut.)

Narrator: Pretty soon, the crocodile returned from his swim.
There was no one around.

Crocodile: All this swimming has made me hungry. I think it's time to open my bag and eat the surprise.
(He begins to untie the bag.)
I am such a clever crocodile.
This morning all I had was a little fish and now I have a...

29

Grandmother and Boy: *(They yell.)*
Surprise!

Narrator: The python swallowed
the crocodile in one gulp!
At last, all the people and animals
in the village were safe
from the not-so-clever crocodile.

FROM THE AUTHOR

Once I met a crocodile who invited me to come closer, but a voice inside me shouted, "No!" I'm very glad I trusted that little voice, so I could write this story!

Richard Vaughan

FROM THE ILLUSTRATOR

I live in Australia with my wife, daughter, and two sons. I enjoy rock-climbing and painting wildlife. Animals are one of my favourite subjects to illustrate.

Kelvin Hawley